To all curious, funny, caring, joyful, kind
and simply wonderful Boys. — NV

Copyright © 2023 by Sourcebooks
Text by Susanna Leonard Hill
Illustrations by Natalie Vasilica
Cover and internal design © 2023 by Sourcebooks

The art was first sketched roughly on paper, then detailed in Procreate on iPad. The artwork was painted digitally in Procreate and Photoshop, mostly using native Procreate brushes (my favorite brush is 6B pencil), as well as a few selected brushes designed by artists I admire: Lucy Fleming, Lynn Chen, and Max Ulichney.

Published by Sourcebooks Wonderland, an imprint of Sourcebooks Kids
P.O. Box 4410, Naperville, Illinois 60567–4410
(630) 961-3900
sourcebookskids.com

Cataloging-in-Publication Data is on file with the Library of Congress.

Source of Production: Phoenix Color, Hagerstown, Maryland, United States of America
Date of Production: September 2022
Run Number: 5024609

Printed and bound in the United States of America.
PHC 10 9 8 7 6 5 4 3 2 1

What Little BOYS Are Made Of

A Modern Nursery Rhyme

Words by **Susanna Leonard Hill**

Pictures by **Natalie Vasilica**

What are little boys made of?
What makes them who they are?
Snips and snails and puppy-dogs' tails?

AHAD

It's more than that by far!

Little boys are dreamers with incredible ideas!
Their imaginations are ever soaring,
heroes defending, lions roaring,
from sea to space, always exploring.

What will they think up next?

Little boys ask questions about everything they see.
What makes waves roll in and out?
How do seeds know when to sprout?
So much for boys to learn about,

and wonder at their world!

Little boys are loving 'cause compassion is the way.
They take the time to show they care.
Forever ready to give and share,
they try their best to make things fair.

Little boys are kind.

Little boys are helpers,
and boys will also pitch in

so dependable and true,
'cause it's just the thing to do.

Little boys are made of fun, warm hearts, and sticky hands.
They roll down a hillside, spin like a top,
make up a play, or read, dance, hop.
Chase after bubbles until they pop!

They find joy in every day.

Little boys are different, each one loved for who they are.
Whether gentle, bold, quiet, tall,
loud, outgoing, shy, or small.
Even in between, this applies to all:

Little boys are special.

Little boys are welcoming to anyone they meet.
When they're playing, joking, or at rest,
they're loyal pals through any test.
Friends help each other be their best,

so as a group they shine.

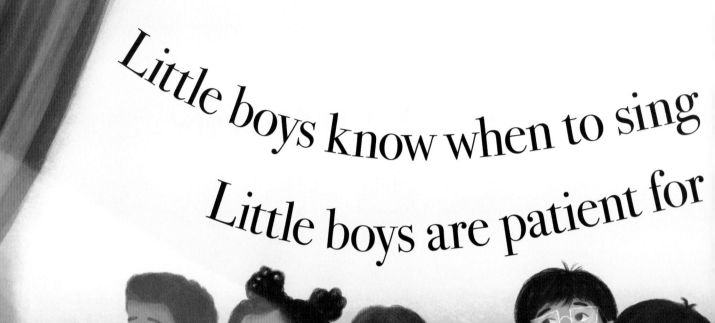

Little boys know when to sing

Little boys are patient for

and when to hum along:
the chance to sing their song.

Little boys are eager to try anything they can.
Sports, adventure, conservation,
theater participation,
cooking, teaching, excavation—

boys have open minds.

Little boys know it's okay to let their feelings out,
because it's brave to show their tears,
their secret wishes and their fears,
their ups and downs throughout the years.

Little boys feel deeply.

Little boys make waves, and their choices cause a splash.
Whether left or right, forward, back,
they pick the path they want to track.
For every act, its own impact.

Their decisions matter.

Little boys keep going. They

And even if they're not the best,

give everything they've got.
they give it their best shot.

Little boys might make mistakes, but they try and try again.
They are learning on-the-go,
and get better as they grow,
'cause through it all they always know—

they're ready for what's next.

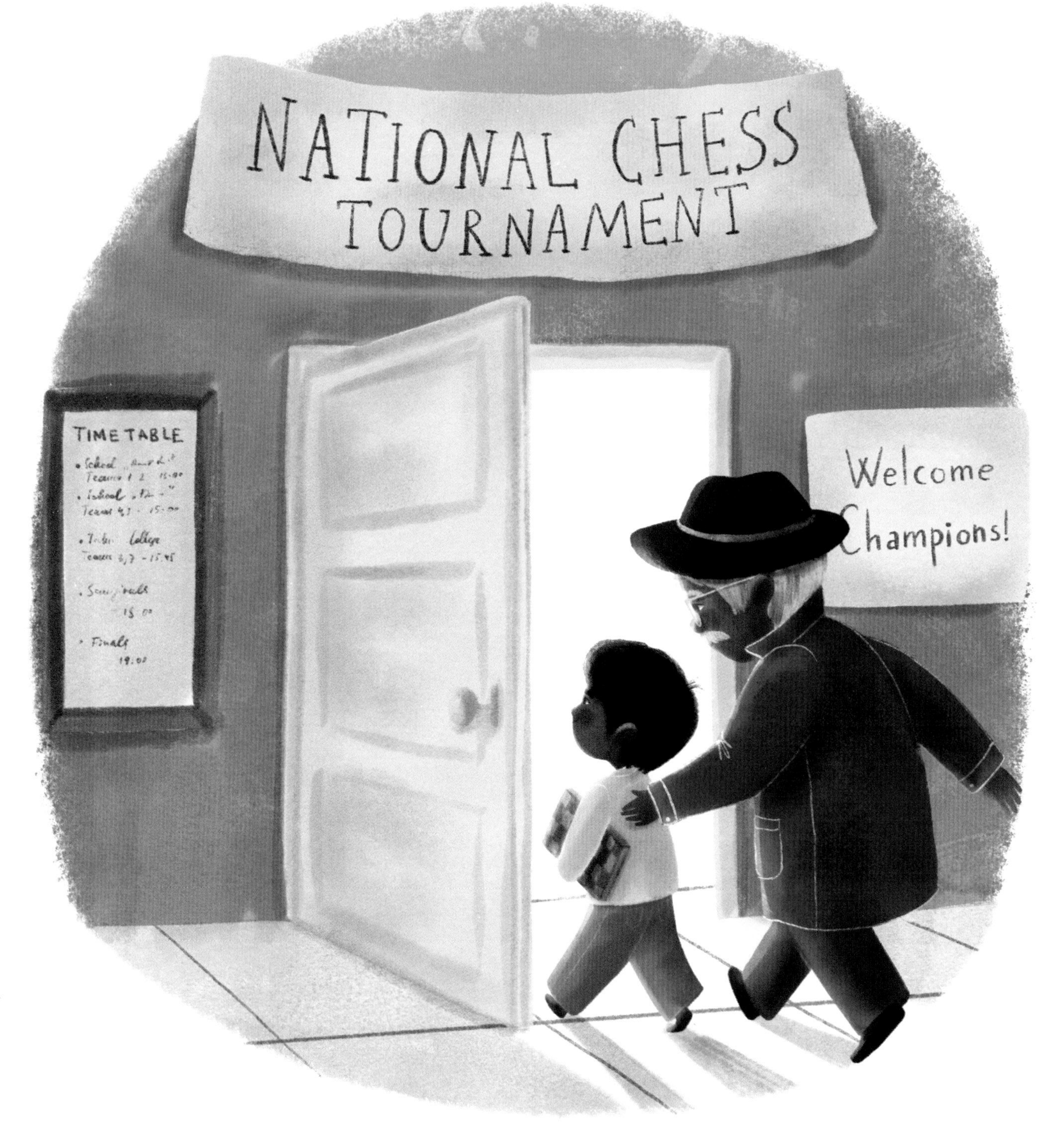
NATIONAL CHESS TOURNAMENT
TIME TABLE
Welcome Champions!

What are little boys made of?
The truest answer is:
There is no single recipe.
Be the boy you want to be!

Little boys are made of dreams

and endless possibility...

I AM HELPFUL
I AM DETERMINED
I CAN DO ANYTHING
I HAVE AN IMPACT
I AM ENOUGH!
I AM LOVED